EVEN MONSTERS NEED HAIRCUTS

Matthew McElligott

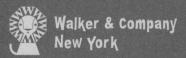

Walker & Company
New York

To Christy and Anthony, and to Frank Hodge,
who for twenty-seven years faithfully opened his store every
full moon so the monsters could come in and pick out a book

First published in the United States of America in August 2010 by
Walker Publishing Company, Inc., a division of Bloomsbury Publishing, Inc.
www.bloomsburykids.com

For information about permission to reproduce selections from this book, write to
Permissions, Walker BFYR, 175 Fifth Avenue, New York, New York 10010

Library of Congress Cataloging-in-Publication Data
McElligott, Matthew.
Even monsters need haircuts / by Matthew McElligott. — 1st U.S. ed.
p.   cm.
Summary: At night under a full moon, a child operates a barber shop
with a monstrous clientele.
ISBN 978-0-8027-8819-1 (hardcover) • ISBN 978-0-8027-8822-1 (reinforced)
[1. Monsters—Fiction. 2. Barbers—Fiction.] I. Title.
PZ7.M478448Ev 2010   [E]—dc22   2009029916

Illustrations created with ink, pencil, and digital techniques
Typeset in Aunt Mildred
Book design by Nicole Gastonguay

Printed in China by Printplus Limited, Shenzhen, Guangdong
2 4 6 8 10 9 7 5 3 1 (hardcover)
2 4 6 8 10 9 7 5 3 1 (reinforced)

All papers used by Bloomsbury Publishing, Inc., are natural, recyclable products
made from wood grown in well-managed forests. The manufacturing processes
conform to the environmental regulations of the country of origin.

My dad is a barber.
I like to watch him work.
I'm a barber too.

Tonight will be a full moon. I'll need to get to bed early.

Just before midnight, I hear a soft
tapping sound.
    Vlad is waiting for me at the window.

I grab my pack and climb down the tree. Together, we cross the fields into town.

I am not allowed out of the house alone.

But I am not alone. Vlad is with me.

Soon we arrive at the alley behind the shop. I have a skeleton key.

I unpack my supplies. The rotting tonic, horn polish, and stink wax go on the counter. The shamp-*ewww* goes next to the sink.

I tuck the moon powder into my pocket, right next to my tangling brush. I'm ready to begin.

Around twelve thirty, Igor wanders in.

By one o'clock, the shop is full.
It's going to be a busy night.

Some customers are easy.

Some are more difficult.

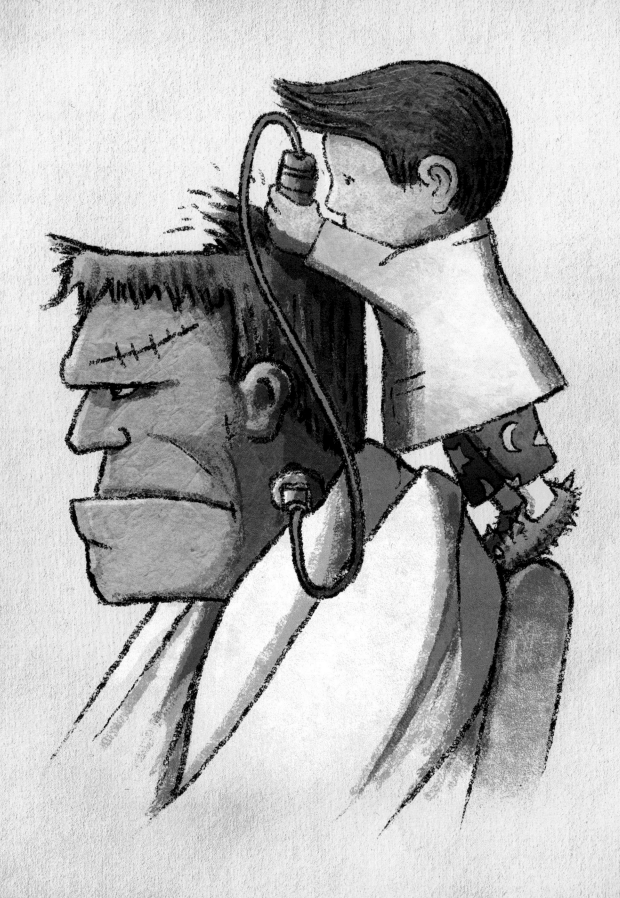

Some always get the same thing.

Some always want to try something new.

And with some customers, it's tough to know exactly what they want.

Things are going well. Everyone is
getting along. And then it happens.
There is a knock at the front door.
No one ever knocks on the front door.
They all know to come in the back.
Who could it be?

It is a customer. A *human* customer.

We have never had a human customer before.

What are we going to do?

Nobody moves as the man walks to the
barber chair.

I am nervous. More nervous than I have
ever been. And then he asks me . . .

"Can you take a little off the top?"

We all have a good laugh over that one.

The sun will be up soon, and the monsters have to go. We sweep up the shop.

We flip back the pictures and turn out
the lights. It's important that we don't
leave *anything* behind.

Some of the guys give me a ride
home.
"See you next month!" I shout.

Soon my dad will be waking up
to go to work. He has his own
customers to take care of.

After all, even humans need haircuts.

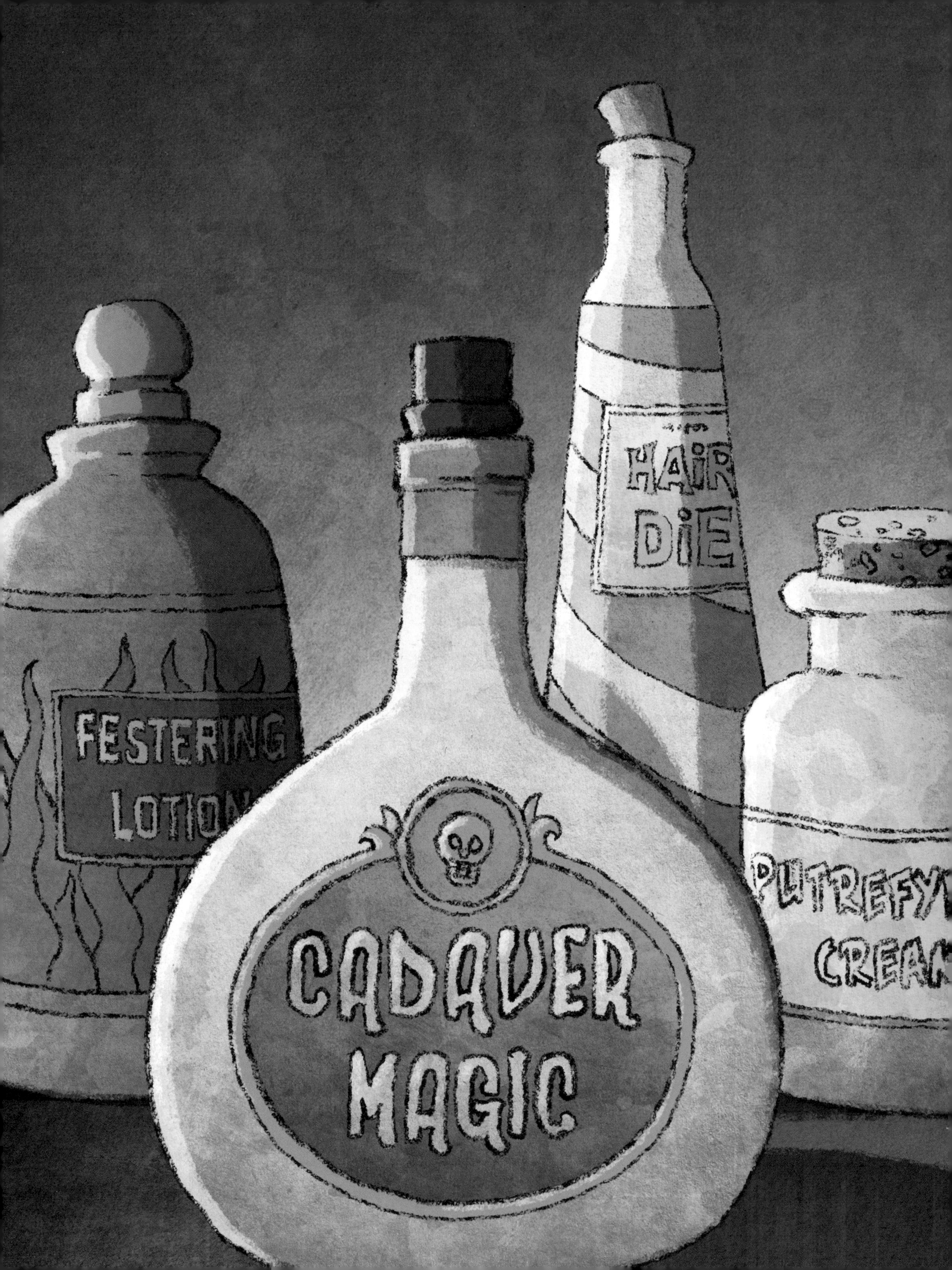
HAIR
DIE
FESTERING
LOTION
CADAVER
MAGIC
PUTREFY
CREAM